Wally,
the
Unlikely Hero

Mark Bessermin

Illustrated by Gale A. Smith

ISBN 978-1-63874-780-2 (paperback)
ISBN 978-1-63874-782-6 (hardcover)
ISBN 978-1-63874-781-9 (digital)

Christian Faith Publishing
832 Park Avenue
Meadville, PA 16335
www.christianfaithpublishing.com

Printed in the United States of America

I will give thanks to thee, for I am
fearfully and wonderfully made.

—Psalm 139:14a

Foreword

Mark Bessermin himself is a kid favorite. As a teacher and an architect, he always combines creativity and purpose as he uses his talents to glorify God. He is a true artist that is skilled in painting and writing, and he really shines when it comes to children. For years, he has been affectionately known as "Mr. B" in our local Christian school. The kids always cheer whenever Mr. B's name is mentioned. His jokes, compliments, teasing, and storytelling fill the classrooms with extra joy. No one could be more of a natural when it comes to teaching a useful lesson and making the world come alive to kids in a book than Mark Bessermin.

I encourage you to find a comfortable place to relax, grab some listening ears, and be ready for a treat. Read this book to your circle of friends, big and small, and Mark will lift your spirits, build your character, and take your imagination on a journey. Enjoy it, and buy another for a friend. Thank you, Mark Bessermin, for blessing us all with your gift. The world is better for it.

With much respect and love,

Pastor Ken Peters

Wally was born just this side of daybreak, a time when everything was magical…a time when everything seemed rose-petal soft and morning-glory sweet! He was born in Mama and Papa's beaver lodge, right in the middle of Amber Pond.

Wally's Mama and Papa had created Amber Pond by cutting down Birch and Alder trees along Babbling Brook. By making a beaver dam, they turned a portion of Babbling Brook into a quiet restful place; a place where their friends from the forest could fish and swim and a place where they could raise a family. And so here, Wally was born to a loving Mama and Papa!

That morning, as the sun crept up the side of the lodge, it tried to peak inside at the newborn baby. Its warm light shone on Wally's little face!

"Oh Papa!" Mama declared. "Look how the sun shines on this little one! I know in my heart that someday he is going to fulfill a great purpose!"

"I couldn't agree more!" Papa beamed.

Later that day, Papa stepped outside of the lodge for a breath of fresh air and to greet his neighbors.

"Hey, Mr. Beaver," Pete the kingfisher yelled, "when do we get to see your baby?"

"Soon," Papa said, "very soon!"

Everyone had come to see the new baby, even King John the Elk and Queen Emma the Eagle. Horace the Skunk was there along with Robin the Robin who was so excited she could hardly contain herself! And Mac and Bert (short for Roberta), those pesky Magpies, were there too.

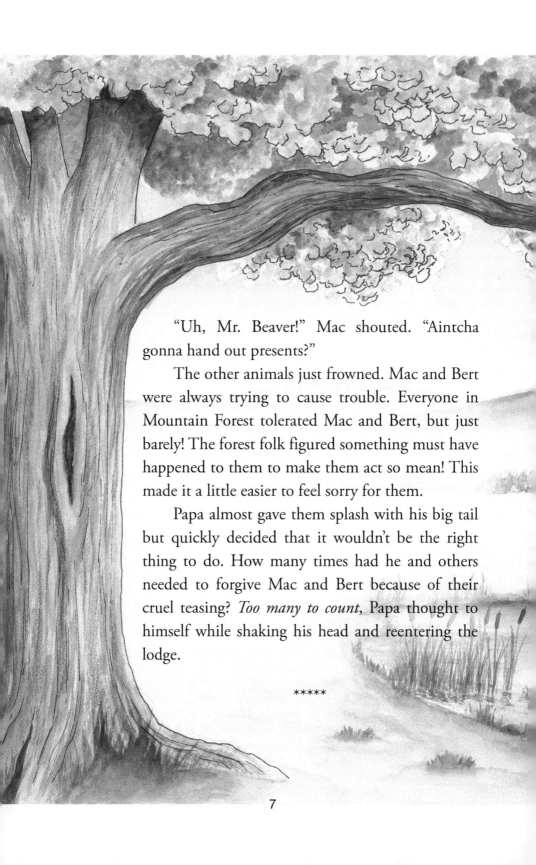

"Uh, Mr. Beaver!" Mac shouted. "Aintcha gonna hand out presents?"

The other animals just frowned. Mac and Bert were always trying to cause trouble. Everyone in Mountain Forest tolerated Mac and Bert, but just barely! The forest folk figured something must have happened to them to make them act so mean! This made it a little easier to feel sorry for them.

Papa almost gave them splash with his big tail but quickly decided that it wouldn't be the right thing to do. How many times had he and others needed to forgive Mac and Bert because of their cruel teasing? *Too many to count*, Papa thought to himself while shaking his head and reentering the lodge.

*****

As time went on, and Wally grew big enough to venture outside, he was allowed to swim in the water around the lodge with Mama keeping a close watch on him to make sure he didn't go very far. Mama loved Wally very much, and Wally loved Mama with all his heart!

One day, Papa came home from working in Mountain Forest. That evening, he whispered something to Mama, and Mama nodded.

"Son," Papa said grinning, "how would you like to go with me tomorrow and look at Mountain Forest and Peaceful Valley?"

"Oh, Mama, may I?" Wally asked with eyes bulging.

"Yes, son, it's time," Mama said smiling.

Wally hardly slept that night. He was so thrilled!

The next morning, Papa had barely opened one eye when Wally chirped, "I'm ready, Pops!"

Papa felt proud to see the way his young son was ready to face the world! And yet at the same time, he wished he could get just…ten…more…minutes of sleep!

Mama got up and made her "men" a hearty breakfast of
Birch pancakes with Maple syrup and a generous helping of
Alder "fork" sausages.

After the "men" had their fill, they both kissed Mama "goodbye" and thanked her for the yummy breakfast.

They dove into the water together with one...big...splash!

Boys will be boys, Mama thoughtfully sighed to herself as she sent her love along with them.

Arriving at the top, Papa and Wally stood at the edge of Mountain Forest, taking in the view.

"Oh Papa!" Wally shrieked while jumping with glee. "This is wonderful!"

"Yes," Papa proclaimed as he put his arm on Wally's shoulder, "Mountain Forest is a wonderful place. We must always care for it and our friends and family who live here. Now, son, look behind you."

As Wally turned, Papa heard him take in a deep breath, for down below, through the draw, was Peaceful Valley.

"Oh, Papa, it's beautiful," Wally whispered.

Papa too was struck with awe when he and Mama saw Mountain Forest and Peaceful Valley for the first time. It really didn't matter how many times Papa had seen the beauty here; he was always humbled by it.

"This is why we built our home here," Papa explained. "When we saw Babbling Brook for the first time, we asked if we might build a pond here, and it gurgled an excited, 'Yes!'"

That was the beginning of a wonderful summer for Wally as he worked alongside Papa. Wally was taught how to build a solid beaver dam by cutting trees down and tightly packing them with mud. He also learned how useful his sharp teeth and large flat tail were in making the dam much stronger.

By the end of summer, Papa and Wally were pleased at what they had accomplished. Papa was also proud of how quickly his son had learned all the skills he had taught him.

As autumn approached, the leaves turned beautiful colors of yellow, orange, and crimson. Wally understood that he would be starting school soon. He was excited about this new adventure but also a little afraid. You see, Mac and Bert would leave Wally alone as long as Papa was nearby. But now at school, he would be without Papa!

On the first day, Wally caught up with his best friends, Pete the Kingfisher, Horace the Skunk, and Robin the Robin.

"Hi, guys, isn't this exciting?" Wally asked.

"Hi, guys, isn't this exciting?" Mac and Bert mimicked in the tree above them, laughing hysterically between themselves!

"Don't pay any attention to them, Wally," Robin encouraged, "they're just plain mean!"

Later at recess, Mac and Bert's teasing grew worse!

"Hey, ping-pong paddle!" they mocked, making fun of Wally's tail. "Don't you wish you had a beautiful tail like ours?"

Wally sadly hung his head. He had never thought his tail ugly, at least before now. Then, to make things worse, on the way home, Mac and Bert really hurt his feelings!

"Hey, bucktooth, smile! We want to take your picture!"

Wally ran home, crying all the way.

"What happened?" Mama asked Pete and Robin when Wally arrived home in tears.

Frowning, they answered, "Mac and Bert called Wally 'bucktooth' and 'ping-pong paddle' at school today."

As Pete and Robin looked on, Mama gently led Wally inside.

When they had entered the lodge, Mama sat on the big Birch rocking chair and lifted Wally onto her lap. Softly, she spoke, "Oh, honey, everyone, not just your Papa and I, love you just the way you are! When you were born, I felt that you were specially made and that someday, you would fulfill a great purpose that only you could because of who you are, and I know you will fulfill the reason why you were born."

A tear rolled down Wally's face as he mustered up a smile. He then drifted off to sleep as Mama rocked him in her sweet embrace.

As time passed, Wally heard many more of these teasing remarks from Mac and Bert, but he began to realize that if he allowed them to see that their words hurt him, it would only encourage them to do it more!

25

Wally was growing up both on the outside and the inside.
He wasn't sure if Mac and Bert ever would!

*****

26

Winter and spring came and departed. Also, Mama and Papa were getting older and wanted to move down into Peaceful Valley where it was warmer.

"Wally," Papa said, "Amber Pond is yours now. Remember what I always say; protect your home and your loved ones. That is what makes this a special place."

Wally nodded in agreement as he waved goodbye.

King John and Queen Emma came by to thank Mama and Papa for making Amber Pond and for being such good neighbors. Pete, Horace, and Robin were there too. Wally was glad to have such good friends! He was also grateful that Mac and Bert weren't around on this sad occasion and wondered what caused them to be such unkind neighbors.

Now on his own, Wally decided to enlarge Amber Pond by cutting down the smaller trees near the edge of the water.

"Why are you doing that?" Pete asked with a look of amazement on his face. He wasn't complaining, mind you, because he knew a bigger pond meant bigger fish for him! "Yum, yum," he said, not realizing he was thinking out loud!

Wally chuckled. "Is that all you think about?"

Pete laughed too! "Well, why are you making it bigger?" Pete quizzed again.

"This summer seems to be starting earlier this year, and the pond is quickly drying up," Wally replied, obviously concerned.

"You're right," Pete agreed, "this summer is already a hot one!"

Little did they know how hot that summer was going to get!

A few weeks later, lightning struck, causing a fire that quickly spread through the dry grass and twigs. All the animals became alarmed when they smelled the smoke but couldn't see the fire. It was above them, out of sight on the other side of the ridge, above Amber Pond. Suddenly, they heard a crackling noise, and then saw flames jump from the ridge onto the tops of the trees…their trees; their *homes!*

"What do we do? What do we do?" they all cried out.

Wally quickly remembered what his Mama had told him to do in case of a fire. "Dive into the water and get into the lodge. There you will be safe." *But what about the others?* he thought. *What about my friends and neighbors?*

Wally had an idea. "Quickly, everyone!" Wally shouted. "I'm going to take you underwater into my house! There you'll be safe!"

One by one, as they held their breaths, Wally guided each underwater and up into the beaver lodge until they were all safe and sound!

"Where are Mac and Bert?" Pete asked nervously.

Realizing they were missing, Wally headed outside. He noticed Mac and Bert on the far side of the pond!

"Help us!" they cried. "Don't let us burn, please!" Just then, a spark landed on Mac's beautiful tail feathers, and they immediately caught on fire!

Mac squealed, "Somebody help me!"

Wally didn't even think twice. He swam to Mac with the speed of a powerboat and, with one swift splash of his tail, put the fire out! A grateful Mac and Bert accepted Wally's kind offer to join the others in the safety of his house.

King John and Queen Emma swiftly escaped the flames after they were assured that their friends were out of harm's way!

Once they were all safely inside, Wally started to leave his home.

Everyone screamed, "Where are you going? Don't go! It's safe in here!"

"But I must try and put the fire out," he said. "I have to save Mountain Forest and Peaceful Valley." Without any hesitation, he dove back into the water!

Meanwhile, the animals safely inside the beaver lodge saw the orange glow of the fire through the tiny cracks between the logs. They knew they were safe because they were surrounded by water. Also, they could hear Wally outside splashing water on the lodge, just in case a drifting spark should fall upon it. Feeling certain the lodge and his friends were no longer in danger, Wally quickly swam to shore.

He became alarmed when he saw the fire jumping from treetop to treetop! He thought, *If only I could cut those trees down and make them fall into the pond. That would put the fires out!*

Like a chainsaw, his razor-sharp teeth quickly cut down all the trees that were on fire, and they fell into the pond, the pond that Wally had made large enough just this year! Wally worked hard all night until all the fires were finally out. If the fire had moved past Amber Pond, it could have raced down the mountainside and destroyed Peaceful Valley!

Wally saved Mountain Forest and Peaceful Valley!

The next morning, a worried Mama and Papa came up to Amber Pond and called for Wally in the lodge.

"We're in here," those inside cried out. "Wally saved us!"

Mama and Papa helped them all outside while King John and Queen Emma began searching for Wally.

Joining the search, Mama yelled out, "*Wally!* Wally, where are you?"

Together they looked over and under burnt logs. It was Queen Emma with her sharp eyes who spotted him first! He was so badly burned that he looked like just another log! To their relief, Wally was going to be just fine!

41

Everyone gathered around as Mama carefully held Wally in her arms.

King John approached and knelt down before Wally. He gracefully bowed his head to him. While the others quietly watched, King John took the crown from his own head and placed it on Wally's.

"Wally, *you* are the true king of this forest!" declared King John.

As grateful friends and family looked on, an exhausted Wally began drifting off to sleep in the comfort of his mother's arms. It was then that he recalled Mama's words from long ago…

"You were created to fulfill a great purpose… I love you just the way you are!"

About the Author

Mark Bessermin, also affectionately known as "Mr. B." to students and parents alike, became a volunteer teacher's aide after retiring to help middle school students, junior high students, and high school students alike. He endeared himself to these folks with his humor and impromptu story telling which often included actual students in his stories. This is how "Wally, The Unlikely Hero" came to be. This book was the precursor to "Northwest Tall Tales, Short Stories, And Other Rare Ramblings", which was self-published by his writer's group, the "Northwest Writers Group."

CPSIA information can be obtained
at www.ICGtesting.com
Printed in the USA
LVHW071549020522
717709LV00019B/1085

9 781638 747802